Min Makes a Machine

More I Like to Read® Books
by Emily Arnold McCully

3, 2, 1, Go!

"This succeeds both as entertainment and instruction; the pachyderms'
social interactions and STEM content are a delightful bonus."
—*Booklist*

★ "A sure hit."
—*Kirkus Review* (starred review)

Pete Likes Bunny

"A sympathetic take on a seldom-discussed situation."
—*Kirkus Reviews*

Pete Makes a Mistake

"This spot-on title is perfect for brand new readers."
—*School Library Journal*

Pete Won't Eat

★ "New readers will eat this up."
—*Kirkus Reviews* (starred review)

★ "The illustrations are priceless."
—*School Library Journal* (starred review)

Min Makes a Machine

Emily Arnold McCully

I Like to Read®

HOLIDAY HOUSE • NEW YORK

I Like to Read® books, created by award-winning picture book artists as well as talented newcomers, instill confidence and the joy of reading in new readers.

We want to hear every new reader say, "I like to read!"

Visit our website for flash cards, activities, and more about the series:
www.holidayhouse.com/ILiketoRead
#ILTR
This book has been tested by an educational expert
and determined to be a guided reading level E.

To all problem-solving girls

"Let's play!" called Min.
"Too hot," said Bess.
"Play with somebody else."

"I will make a fan," said Min.

"It's still too hot," said Ann.
"I wish we could swim."

"There is the old pool," said Ann.
"But it has no water," said Bess.

"I will look for water!" said Min.
"I am going home," said Ann.
"This is no fun."

"Look!" called Min.
"I found an old well."

"The water is at the bottom,"
said Bess.

"I will get it out,"
said Min.
Off she went.

Min came back.

She had a long tube.

Next she got
a hose.

Min put glue
on the tube.

Then she put the hose
on the tube.

"We are ready," said Min.
"How?" asked Bess.

Min put the tube
into the well.

"This is the hard part," said Min.

Min turned the tube . . .

and turned . . .

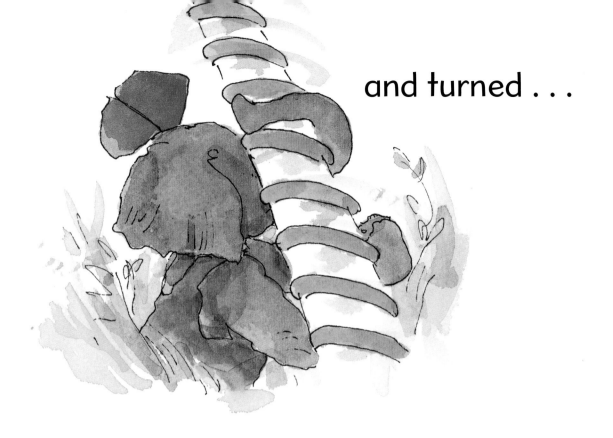

and turned . . .

and turned!

Water came out!

The pool filled up.

Bess and Min got in.

Ann jumped in too.

Splash!